The **Itsy** **Bitsy** **Spider**

The Itsy Bitsy Spider

Classic Nursery Rhymes Retold

Joe Rhatigan

Illustrated by Carolina Farías

MoonDance

The itsy bitsy spider
climbed up the waterspout.
Down came the rain
and washed the spider out.

Out came the sun
and dried up all the rain.
And the itsy bitsy spider
climbed up the spout again.

The silly willy caterpillars
played leapfrog in the trees.
One grabbed two leaves
and floated on the breeze.

The breeze died down,
she sank slowly to the ground.
And landed so softly
she didn't make a sound.

The flitter flutter butterflies
opened up their pretty wings.
They loved to flip and flap
while the grasshopper sings.

They hopped, jumped, and rocked
and did a funny dance.
It was a happy show
for the spiders, bees, and ants.

The creepy-crawly spider
felt left out of the fun.
He sat under a tree
far away from everyone.

The ladybug said, "Hide,
and I will count to ten."
The spider laughed and giggled
and joined his friends again.

The shiny whiny beetle
dug herself a hole.
She filled it up with water
and made a swimming pool.

The tiny ants jumped in,
splashed and had great fun.
The beetle swam around
and gave rides to everyone.

The busy buzzy bees
played jump rope with the worm.
The worm got too dizzy,
and he began to squirm.

The bees picked him up
and flew him up so high.
He did a happy wiggle.
Oh, how he loved to fly!

The winky blinky fireflies
lit up the evening sky.
They tucked in their friends
and sang a lullaby.

The moms and dads made sure
the little ones got hugs.
Now it's time to say good night
to all the silly bugs.

Quarto is the authority on a wide range of topics.
Quarto educates, entertains, and enriches the lives of our readers—
enthusiasts and lovers of hands-on living.
www.quartoknows.com

© 2017 Quarto Publishing Group USA Inc.
Published by MoonDance Press,
an imprint of The Quarto Group
All rights reserved. MoonDance is a registered trademark.

Cover design and layout by Melissa Gerber.

All rights reserved. No part of this book may be reproduced in any form without written permission of the copyright owners. All images in this book have been reproduced with the knowledge and prior consent of the artists concerned, and no responsibility is accepted by producer, publisher, or printer for any infringement of copyright or otherwise, arising from the contents of this publication. Every effort has been made to ensure that credits accurately comply with information supplied. We apologize for any inaccuracies that may have occurred and will resolve inaccurate or missing information in a subsequent reprinting of the book.

MoonDance

6 Orchard Road, Suite 100
Lake Forest, CA 92630
quartoknows.com
Visit our blogs at quartoknows.com

Reproduction of work for study or finished art is permissible. Any art produced or photomechanically reproduced from this publication for commercial purposes is forbidden without written consent from the publisher, MoonDance Press.

Printed in China
3 5 7 9 10 8 6 4 2